D1249448

©LEVEL-5/YWP.

In accordance with the U.S. Copyright Act of 1976, the scanning, uploading, and electronic sharing of any part of this book without the permission of the publisher is unlawful piracy and theft of the author's intellectual property. If you would like to use material from the book (other than for review purposes), prior written permission must be obtained by contacting the publisher at permissions@hbgusa.com. Thank you for your support of the author's rights.

Little, Brown and Company

Hachette Book Group
1290 Avenue of the Americas, New York, NY 10104
Visit us at lb-kids.com

LB kids is an imprint of Little, Brown and Company.
The LB kids name and logo are trademarks of Hachette Book Group, Inc.

The publisher is not responsible for websites (or their content) that are not owned by the publisher.

First Edition: October 2016

ISBN 978-0-316-39621-9

10 9 8 7 6 5 4 3 2 1

PHX

Printed in the United States of America

SEEK AND FIND

Written by Justus Lee
Art by Kevin Meyers

LITTLE, BROWN & COMPANY
LB kids

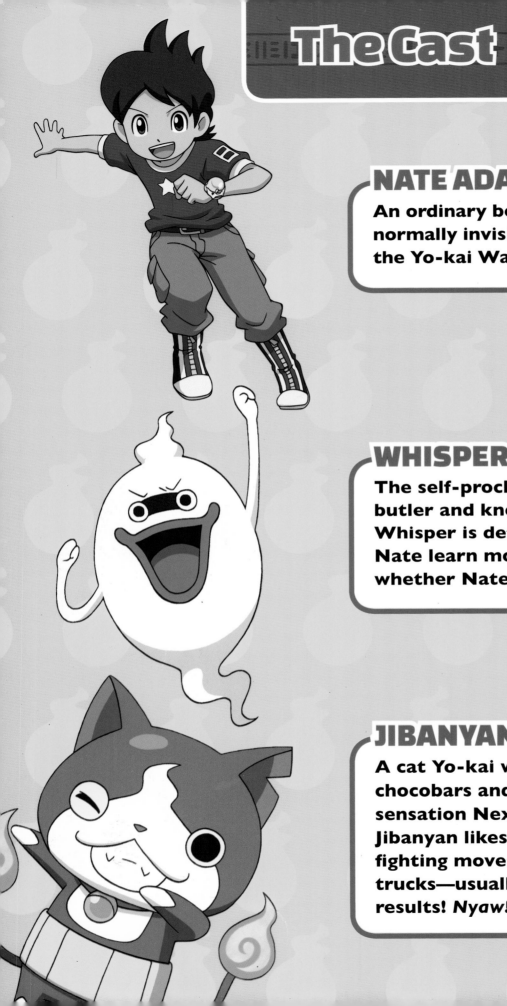

The Cast

NATE ADAMS

An ordinary boy who can see the normally invisible Yo-kai using the Yo-kai Watch!

WHISPER

The self-proclaimed "Yo-kai butler and know-it-all," Whisper is determined to help Nate learn more about Yo-kai—whether Nate wants to or not!

JIBANYAN

A cat Yo-kai who loves to eat chocobars and admires the pop sensation Next HarMEOWny, Jibanyan likes to practice his fighting moves on passing trucks—usually with painful results! *Nyaw!*

The Story

One normal summer day, an average fifth-grader named Nathan Adams, or Nate as he likes to be called, comes across an old and strange capsule vending machine deep in the mountains. He puts in a coin and opens the sealed rock capsule to discover—a Yo-kai named Whisper!

Whisper gives Nate a Yo-kai Watch that allows him to see hidden Yo-kai all over town.

Nate's life will never be the same!

Mount Wildwood

Ever since Whisper gave Nate the Yo-kai Watch, Nate can see strange and mysterious creatures everywhere!

CAN YOU SPOT:

- Enerfly
- Enefly
- Betterfly
- Peppillon
- Negatibuzz
- Beetler
- Buhu
- Cadin
- a golden bug
- Nate's net
- the capsule machine
- Whisper's capsule
- the Yo-kai Watch

A Busy Intersection

This intersection is bustling with people today, and Nate wants to see if there are Yo-kai roaming around here! Is that a cat or a Yo-kai?

CAN YOU SPOT:

- Thornyan
- Dianyan
- Sapphinyan
- Emenyan
- Topanyan
- Rubinyan
- Baddinyan
- Robonyan
- Shogunyan
- a chocobar
- Jibanyan's EXTRA-fuzzy belly warmer
- fatty tuna
- a Next HarMEOWny poster
- Jibanyan's metallic collar

Nate's Bedroom

Was Nate's room always this messy, or is this the work of a Yo-kai? Nate needs your help to clean up this mess!

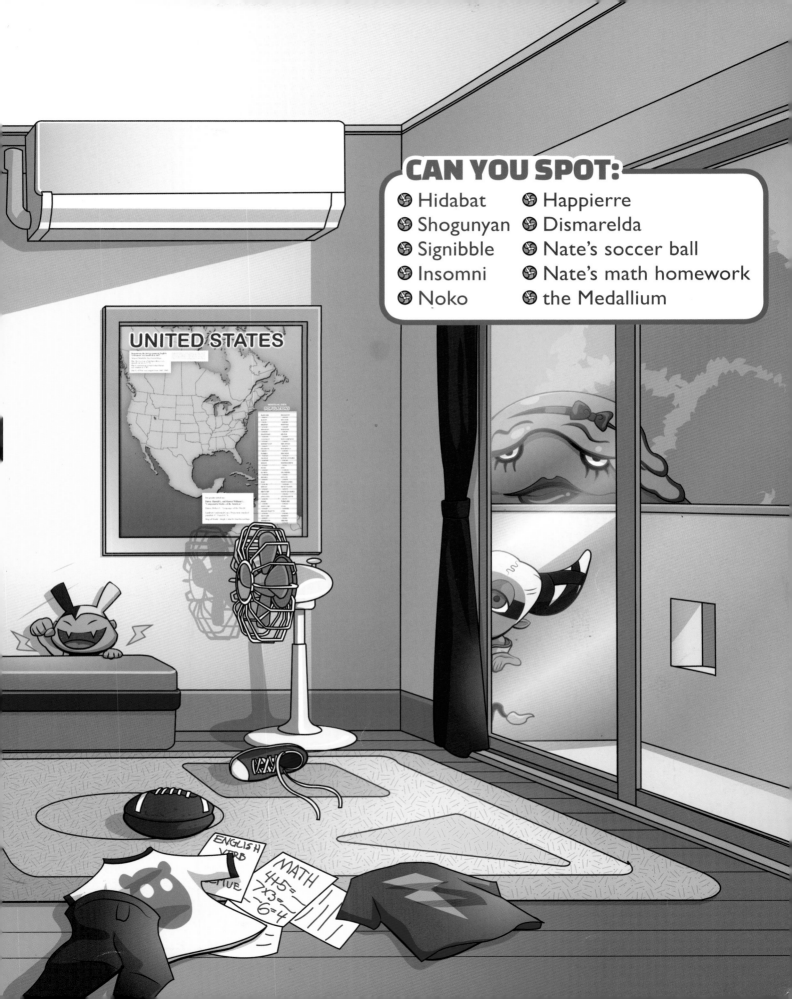

CAN YOU SPOT:

- Hidabat
- Shogunyan
- Signibble
- Insomni
- Noko
- Happierre
- Dismarelda
- Nate's soccer ball
- Nate's math homework
- the Medallium

Classroom Disaster!

Something strange is definitely going on in the classroom. Nate's friends are acting strange, and Nate knows who are responsible!

CAN YOU SPOT:

- Bear
  inspirited by Rockabelly
- Katie
  inspirited by Blazion
- Eddie
  inspirited by Roughraff
- the teacher, Mr. Johnson,
  inspirited by Wazzat
- Baddinyan
- Wiglin, Steppa, Rhyth
- Daiz
- Whisper's Yo-kai Pad
- a flower pot
- Nate's backpack with
  the Medallium in it

Everymart

Nate needs a snack after that classroom catastrophe.
Perhaps Everymart will be Yo-kai free.

CAN YOU SPOT:

- Fidgephant
- Mirapo
- Hungramps
- Tattletell
- Manjimutt
- Cheeksqueek
- Walkappa
- a roe rice ball
- a can of Y-cola
- soul tea
- curry bread
- ramen cup
- comic books

Buy One Get One Free

mogmog Burgers

Maybe a snack isn't the right way to go, but a full meal sounds like the right idea for Nate! Hey, look! There are two Yo-kai figuring out what to order!

CAN YOU SPOT:

- Komasan
- Komajiro
- Whisper
- Buhu
- Jibanyan
- an apple pie
- a super-deluxe hamburger
- French fries
- a salad
- XXL soda
- chicken nuggets
- soft-serve ice cream (Oh my swirls!)
- fruit
- cookies

A Night in the Park

The sun goes down, the moon goes up, and Nate sees even more weird things happening around him at the park!

CAN YOU SPOT:

- Dimmy
- Negatibuzz
- Timidevil
- Tengloom
- Suspicioni
- Ake
- Leadoni
- Cupistol
- Rattelle
- Manjimutt
- chairs
- food stand
- poodle
- lamppost

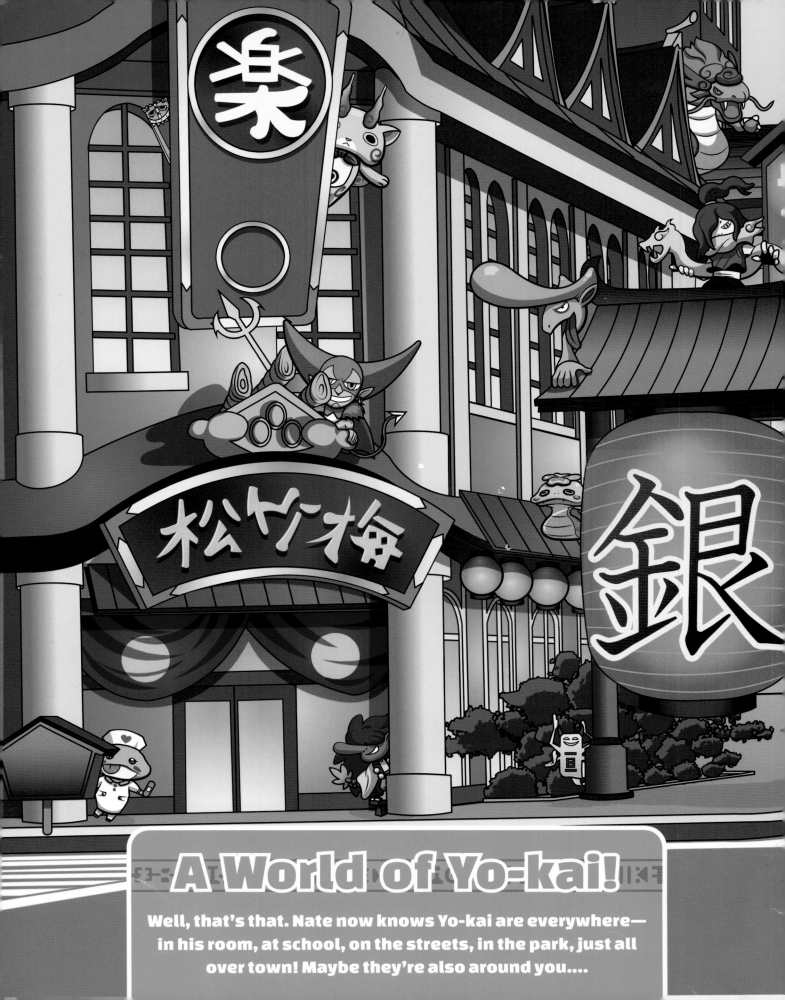

A World of Yo-kai!

Well, that's that. Nate now knows Yo-kai are everywhere—
in his room, at school, on the streets, in the park, just all
over town! Maybe they're also around you....

CAN YOU SPOT:

- Kyubi
- Venoct
- Jibanyan
- Whisper
- Babblong
- Illoo
- K'mon-K'mon
- Blizzaria
- Beelzebold
- Tengu
- Dragon Lord
- Blazion
- Noko
- Roughraff
- Nurse Tongus
- Lie-In Heart
- So-Sorree
- Dracunyan
- Komasan
- Komajiro

Answer Key

Mount Wildwood

A Busy Intersection

Nate's Bedroom

Classroom Disaster!

Everymart

mogmog Burger

A Night in the Park

A World of Yo-Kai!

Is this the end? Of course not! There are a few more things hidden for you to find! Go back for another look and see if you can spot:

8 chocobars

7 Whispers

4 Yo-kai Medals

2 Yo-kai Pads

5 Jibanyans

1 Watch face

And remember! You are looking for the Watch face icon in the scenes! The Watch face icons in the lists do not count!

E LEE   FLT
Lee, Justus,
Yo-kai watch :seek and find /

DISCARD

11/16